Copyright ©

ISBN: 978-1-6781-2268-3

Matt Shaw Publications

All rights reserved. This book or any portion thereof may not be reproduced or used in any manner whatsoever without the express written permission of the publisher except for the use of brief quotations in a book review.

The characters in this book are purely fictitious.

Any likeness to persons living or dead is purely coincidental.

www.facebook.com/mattshawpublications

THE

FUNHOUSE

MATT SHAW

BOY MEETS GIRL

1

You wouldn't have thought it was the middle of August. The rain beat down on the quiet streets outside the restaurant. Occasionally a car passed by with its lights illuminating the wet ground with a shimmering effect; pretty when looked upon from beneath shelter.

The night-air was crisp with a chill in the air which, by morning, would freeze the puddles over and make for treacherous driving conditions for the morning commuters. An out of season cold-front brought in from overseas, according to the weather reports. The unwelcome effects of Global Warming, changing the weather systems which were considered "normal" for this time of the year.

In the restaurant, music quietly played over the speaker system hanging from the four corners of the room. That, with the gentle chitter-chatter of feasting customers and you could barely hear the sound of the sheets of rain lashing against the glass windows. An open fire - a centrepiece in the expensive eatery - blazed away too, which also helped those dining forget about the misery outside.

Despite the weather, the restaurant was running at capacity with the waiting staff rushed off their feet as they served the tables. Some tables were group bookings, friends who'd just decided to get together after to celebrate "whatever". Other tables were with husbands and wives, husbands and mistresses, partners and even work colleagues who'd decided to come out after a particularly stressful day in the office, wherever that was. Then, of course, there were the patrons who'd chosen this venue as the perfect location for their "first date". Whether they picked the restaurant because of its reputation as one of the best, or because it was one of the most central in the city was by the by. In Jim's case, as he eye-balled the steep prices on the menu he was thumbing through, it was because it was the only restaurant he really *knew*. If he was eating out it was usually with his friends on a night out and they'd end up in a fast food place, or propped up - drunk - against a kebab van. They never went to a restaurant because it was a waste of money which would be better spent on alcohol. But, having just met his date on the Internet and - looking at her profile - seeing she was used to the finer things in life, he wanted to make a good impression. If the prices were a fair representation of the food they were about to eat, he was about to make a *really* good impression. That being said, had he checked the menu online first, he would have chosen someplace else. He wanted to make a good impression, sure, but at the same time, he also didn't want to max out his credit card.

'Wow. Pricey,' Laura said as she scanned her own copy of the menu.

'I was going to make a comment about the salad being a good choice,' Jim said, half-joking, 'until I saw the price of that.' Usually a restaurant would have "salad" as one of the cheaper options on the menu but, here, it was almost as much as a small steak. Jim presumed the lettuce leaves must have been gold-leaf, or something stupid. Or maybe the chef comes out and bounces salt off his bare elbow, down onto the raw shreds of carrot? Jim had just finished reading about another place in London which had a chef do that. Admittedly it wasn't on salad but, even so, the chef would come out and literally bounce salt off his elbow and onto the diner's steak. And, for the privilege, he'd set an astronomically high price and - worryingly - there were mugs out there who actually thought it was a "good deal".

Laura looked up over the rim of her menu and said, 'We can go somewhere else…'

As much as Jim would have loved to go elsewhere, he wasn't about to be *that* guy either. 'It's fine. Honestly. I knew what the prices were before we got here,' he lied. 'I just wanted to treat you to something nice for a first date.' He added, 'First impressions, and all that.'

Laura smiled. 'So our second date…'

Jim finished her sentence, 'Will be a kebab van.'

'Aren't you worried that bringing me here sets a standard? I might expect this all the time.'

Jim smiled and just hoped that his smile was "enough" to hide his fear. He *hadn't* actually thought about that, and tonight was going to be a big enough hit on his wallet. What if she wanted a second date this week and, what if she wanted to come back here? Aware he was getting ahead of himself, he quickly dismissed the thought. For one, he needed to make it through to a second date and, for another thing, *she* might not have wanted to go out again either. Even if they both wanted it, he could always buy himself some time by saying he was busy for a few days although, what if she meets someone else in those "busy days"? And now he was panicking. *Fuck.* It had been too long since his last girlfriend and he just felt out of practise. He suddenly realised Laura was watching him with a bemused smile on her face.

'Are you okay?' she asked.

He laughed. 'Sorry, I'm just really nervous?'

'You are? Why? Am I scary?'

'It's just been a long time since I've been out with someone.'

'Oh really?'

Jim nodded. 'I was in a long-term relationship and... Well... When that fell apart, I wasn't in a hurry to get out and do it all again, you know?'

'How long was the relationship?'

'Five years.'

'That *is* a long time. You weren't engaged or anything?'

'Nope. Just boyfriend and girlfriend.'

'You didn't want to propose?'

Jim felt his face flush with the direct question. He didn't mind talking about his past. He had nothing to be embarrassed about but, usually, the conversations came out in a more natural way. This felt like he was in a firing line as she rattled off her questions. Still, she asked so... Jim said, 'Not after she slept with my best-friend.' It had hurt at the time, when the truth came to light, but now he was able to just laugh it off and - as such - he couldn't help but chuckle.

'Ah. Yeah. I can see how that would take the shine off a relationship.'

Jim shrugged. 'These things happen.' Eager to learn more about her, he turned the question back to her, 'What about you?'

'What about me what?'

'Been single long?'

'Not quite. I'm actually married. I just get bored. My husband goes away a lot and so, he said I can come out on these evening's out... He just said I have to be home by midnight and let him know I am safe. But, other than that...' When Laura saw Jim's shocked expression, she couldn't hide her laughter. Laura giggled. 'I've been single for a while, yes.'

'You actually had me worried then...'

Laura laughed again. 'I could tell. But, no, I am most definitely single. I guess there's something wrong with me in that I keep scaring people off.' With a cheeky grin, she added, 'Probably my sense of humour.'

'You think?'

A waiter approached from the side with a smile on his face. 'Good evening.'

'Hi…'

'Hello…'

'Can I get you two some drinks?'

2

'You're sure I can't go halves with you? It would make me feel better…'

'Thank you but it is fine.'

A starter, a main and a dessert - not forgetting a few drinks on top of that. Laura had no idea how much the bill had come to, given the fact Jim had hidden the figure from her but, going by the wide-eyed expression on his face, she knew it wasn't cheap. She was right too. With tip included, it had come to just shy of two hundred and fifty pounds which was - Jim believed - the most he'd ever spent on a first date. Whilst it hit him in the wallet hard, he didn't care. Whether she'd had a nice night or not, and he hoped she had, he'd had a *great* night. So, for him, the meal was worth every penny. It also helped that the food was exquisite too, with each mouthful causing a miniature explosion in his tastebuds.

'I feel bad,' Laura said.

'Honestly it's fine but, I appreciate the offer.' He said, 'Anyway it's rude to invite someone on a date and then make them pay for half of it. I invited you here, so I get the bill. If it makes you feel any better, you can invite me out next time and then you can pay.' He flashed her a cheeky smile. It was fair to say his confidence had shot up during the date.

'Oh, was that your not-so-subtle way of saying you'd like to see me again?' Laura asked with a raised eyebrow.

'Of course, I want to see you again. You owe me a meal,' he said, still with that very same grin on his face.

'What if I wait for you to ask me out for a second date?'

'Well, we either go elsewhere, or we offer to wash up for them. Or,' he quickly added, 'we learn how to do a runner as soon as we've eaten.'

'We could do that now,' Laura said as she started to look over her shoulder. 'No one is paying us any attention… We could just get up and run out before the waiter comes back…'

'Miss Gisele?' a voice approached from behind.

'Ah. Too late,' Laura said. She turned to see who'd called her name. The waiter was coming back to the table with both the card machine and the manager. The manager was smiling from cheek to cheek. His name was Victor and, both he and Laura knew one another fairly well. 'Good evening, Victor…'

'Wait, you're on first name terms with the staff?' Jim asked, under his breath but still heard by both Victor and the waiter.

Before Laura could answer him, the waiter presented him with the card machine and said, 'If you would just like to put your card in the machine and follow the instructions…' Jim did as both the waiter and card machine instructed as Victor and Laura seemingly went about having a quick catch-up.

'We have missed you here,' Victor said. 'How is your father?'

'Oh he's fine. He's just been busy recently. You know him.'

'Indeed I do! So much work to do to make this city nice again… Must be rushed off his feet.'

Jim had no idea what they were talking about but smiled and nodded along as though he were a part of what was happening too. He handed the card machine back to the waiter who printed the receipt and tore it off for Jim with a simple, "Thank you". Jim didn't respond as he tried to keep up with the other conversation.

'Well tell your father we were asking after him and, of course, whenever he wants to come in it would be our pleasure to host him again. For free, of course.'

'Thank you. I'll let him know… It was good to see you again.'

'And you, Miss Gisele. Hopefully we will see you again soon.' Victor turned to Jim and nodded his head towards him before adding, 'Good evening.'

'Hello…' Jim said, confused as to what the hell was going on. Before he could ask, Victor and the waiter left the table. He turned his attention to Laura whose face was glowing red. 'Your dad gets to eat here free? I mean… Damn. What do we have to do to get some of that action?'

Laura laughed. 'Become Mayor...'

'Wait, what?'

Jim was still laughing at himself when he entered his small apartment. From Laura's dating profile, he could tell she liked the finer things in life; nice holiday photos on beaches and fancy-looking ski resorts, at parties she looked like she was always dressed immaculately. It was obvious she came from a good background, certainly better than his anyway. That being said, he had *no* idea she was the Mayor's daughter.

Jim closed his front door and switched the hallway light on. He laughed again. It was no wonder she was shocked by the prices if they were usually allowed to eat there for free. Of all the people to meet, it was her. And of all the places to take her, it was the damn restaurant in which they eat for nothing. Fair play to her though because she didn't once bring up her dad, or anything to do with that "world". If anything, when the manager came over, she almost seemed embarrassed by the "secret" coming out.

The whole situation was amusing and Jim knew his work colleagues would get a good kick out of it the next day, when he went into the office, but, at the same time, it was a little depressing too. Her dad was the Mayor. She came from a strong background and clearly money wasn't an issue for them. He had nothing to offer her. Sure, he wasn't on *bad* money but there were still some months where he struggled to make ends meet. With that thought in his mind, Jim walked into his living room. He turned the light on and just stood there in the doorway for a moment.

The room was of a modest size. There was a sofa, a large television hanging on the wall, a games console sitting on an otherwise bare television stand, a coffee table - polished only yesterday - and a bookcase with more films stacked upon it than books. With the ambitious thought of bringing his date back home with him, he'd spent the previous night cleaning up so - it looked pretty nice in there *but*, was it really a standard she would be used to? He would have brought her back but parked up in the carpark he'd instantly been hit with looking for any excuse as to why she couldn't get out of the car. It didn't help that there were broken bottles smashed on the ground outside where the local youths had clearly been bored that evening. Whenever they were bored, shit got smashed. It was just what they did although Jim never understood why. They lived here too so, why would they want to live in a place surrounded by broken glass? It made no sense but, whatever… It was barely fit enough for Jim to live here, let alone for the Mayor's daughter to come here for a fleeting visit, or anything else.

Jim shrugged as he slumped down on his sofa. He kicked his shoes off and put his feet up on the coffee table before he turned the television on. She might not want to see him again but, whatever. It had been nice to get out again. The food was good, the company was great. Whether he never saw or spoke to her again, it hadn't been a wasted evening. It had been nice and, Jim found himself smiling as the evening's events played through his mind once again. He didn't regret spending all that money to take her out. The only thing he regretted was not offering her a night-cap back at his, or another bar someplace else. Well, that and the fact he regretted not trying to kiss her too. Even if she would have said "no" to either, at least he would have tried. Mind you - a sudden thought - would that have tainted an otherwise excellent evening? As various answers to the question came to mind, Jim's phone buzzed from inside his pocket. He reached into his jeans and pulled it out.

On the screen, there was a notification from the dating app on which he'd first met Laura. Perfect timing, he thought. As one date ends, he matches with another - hopefully better suited - lady.

The phone's screen unlocked at the touch of a button and Jim navigated to the dating app. He tapped it open and laughed out loud as a message from Laura popped up in his inbox. He read; she saw they had matched on the app and, as such, she was inviting him out on a date with her. The message pointed out that, as she asked him, it would be her treat.

Jim didn't want to keep her waiting. He quickly tapped out his response. 'I'd love to,' he said. 'Just name a date and place…'

The answer came back in the blink of an eye and simply read, 'Kebab van?' And, next to that, there was a smiling emoji.

BOY LIKES GIRL

3

August was a wash-out. It had rained for ninety percent of the days, just as it had done when Rihanna's "Umbrella" song hit the charts back in 2008. Back then, the sun was meant to be shining and people were meant to be enjoying their summer holidays but whenever her song seemed to play, it brought about dark clouds and rain-storms. This year was much the same, just without her music blasting from speakers across the country. Despite the poor weather, Jim had been having some of his best days.

At work, Jim had finally been given a promotion. It wasn't anything major but "something" was better than "nothing". It was also a promotion which had been dangled in front of him for a few years now and, until they called him into the office to offer it, he was starting to believe it was never *actually* going to materialise. Instead, he was worrying that it was just something they were teasing to keep him working there, instead of looking for another job. There was even a part of him which thought, when they finally gave it, they didn't really *want* him to have it. He felt they were offering it just to shut him up but, to hell with them… Even if that was the case, it didn't matter. Not now he had it, and the little extra money the new position offered.

Jim's personal life was going from strength to strength too. He was still living in his small apartment - albeit with an eye to moving out within the next year - but, now he could actually tell people that he had a girlfriend! He and Laura had been inseparable, despite his earlier concerns that she'd soon get bored with him and find someone else…

To begin with, after each date, he figured that would be it and he wouldn't hear from her again but, each time, she continued to surprise him by replying to his messages. More than that, it was usually Laura who initiated the conversations pretty much as soon as the dates had ended. It was never a lot, just a simple text - within hours of parting company - stating that she was missing him. When their relationship progressed to the next level, those messages changed to picture messages. They were never outwardly rude, just shots teasing nudity and usually accompanied by a cheeky message, such as "thinking about you". Never enough to get her in trouble, should the photos have been leaked, but certainly enough to get Jim hot under the collar.

After a month of seeing each other religiously, Jim relaxed a little into the relationship. He realised, despite his concerns, that she *wasn't* getting bored with him, and *wasn't* about to ditch him for someone better. In fact, he once confessed his early concerns to Laura (when they were in a better position) and she almost seemed offended he'd been having the thoughts.

'You're not still thinking like that, are you?' she'd asked.

There was a massive weight off his shoulders when he was finally able to answer, 'Not anymore.'

'You sure you want to do this?'

'100%.'

'Because, you know, you have *literally* just met her.'

'Actually we've been dating for over a month now.'

'Which really isn't that long.'

'What can I say? When you know, you know.'

'You're crazy.'

'I'm in love.'

'Crazy.'

'Oh so, you don't want to be my best man then?'

'I mean, I didn't say I wouldn't be coming. I'm just making sure you know what you're doing.'

Jim laughed. 'I do.'

'Then, good… Hurry up and buy it so we can get to the pub!'

It was an unseasonably warm September, after a wash-out August. With sunshine scheduled for most of the day, Jim had dragged his best friend Mitch into town. It was a rare day off for both of them and Jim had suggested a couple of pints at one of the bars in town. It was a bar which Laura had introduced him to as, before meeting her, Jim had never known it existed. From the outside it looked like any other over-priced bar in London but, once you went in... Plush seats, table service and - better yet for when the sun did shine down on this shitty little country - a garden up on the roof. The perfect escape from reality where you could quietly sink a couple of ice-cold pints with your nearest and dearest. And that *had* been Jim's plan right up until the moment he passed by the jewellery store and had his attention stolen by the dazzling rings on display. *"I'm going to marry her,"* he'd said.

Mitch, a colleague who worked in the same office, mumbled, 'Did you really just drag me here to help you pick a ring? Or, are we going to get to the pub at some point?'

'Don't rush me. It needs to be the right one.'

Mitch was scanning the various rings on display. More specifically, he was scanning the prices. 'What if she says no? Do you get to return the ring, or does she keep it?'

Jim hadn't thought about it that way. Instead of letting his imagination run wild, he simply said, 'She won't say no.'

'But if she does...'

'Mate, seriously...' Jim pointed out a silver-coloured ring. 'What about that one?' Platinum band with a single diamond stone on the top; elegant, timeless, fucking expensive. Mitch's eyes went straight to the price.

'How much was that fucking pay rise you got with the promotion?'

A nearby store lady, who'd been ear-wigging on the conversation, asked from behind the counter, 'Would you like to take a look?'

Mitch asked, 'Just so we know, can we get a refund if his woman declines his offer?' Before the assistant even had a chance to say anything, Mitch turned to Jim and asked, 'Have you even asked her dad?'

'What are you talking about?'

'Ah man, you really haven't thought this through, have you? You're supposed to get permission.'

'What?!' Jim turned to the assistant in the hope she was going to laugh Mitch's comments off. She didn't. She simply nodded along with him. 'That's right?'

'It is,' she said.

Mitch asked the assistant, 'Okay, can we get our money back if *he* says no?'

4

Mitch wasn't impressed but at least Jim had dropped him off back at his house, instead of just abandoning him in the middle of town. It was Mitch's fault. Had he not mentioned the age-old tradition of getting the father's permission to wed his daughter, Jim would have bought the over-priced ring and they'd both be in the beer garden now, sipping a fresh one. As it was, Jim grabbed the ring (he had twenty-eight days to return it) and said he needed to go round Laura's to see her dad, whilst Laura herself was at work. It was the only day Jim knew for a *fact* that her dad, Mayor David Gisele, would be at home and she wouldn't be so, Jim really didn't want to miss the opportunity.

Now he was sitting in David's office, tucked away in a back room of the large family home in the posh estate, Jim was almost wishing that the opportunity hadn't been there and he was sitting in the pub instead. It was Mitch's fault Jim's heart was racing ten to the dozen. Whilst Jim was fairly confident Laura was going to say "yes" to him, he wasn't sure about David's response. The only good thing was, he'd met the family on a number of occasions now and - to his face at least - they all seemed to like him. Sitting with them around the large dining room table, tucking into a chef-cooked Sunday roast dinner, there was never a time when Jim felt unwelcome, or that he was being judged. The entire family welcomed him with open arms and broad smiles on their faces. In fact, being with them, Jim finally felt as though he were a part of a *real* family.

Jim's own mother had died when he was just five years old. He had come home from school one rainy afternoon and found her hanging from the loft hatch. Her skin was pale but her lips were blue as she gently swung there. Jim didn't scream when he saw her there. Not initially anyway. He just stood there and watched her sway for a minute or two. Then, the screaming started and it felt like it had never really stopped. Not inside.

Jim's father couldn't cope with the suicide. There had been no note, no explanation. There had been no signs that *this* had been coming and - as a result - he blamed himself. If it wasn't his fault, she would have tried to talk to him, wouldn't she? Instead she locked herself in the family home and...

Jim's father hit the bottle hard. It wasn't long after that, he started to hit his son. The drink shifted the blame away from himself and planted it solely on Jim's shoulders. *Look what you made your mother do.*

As soon as Jim was able to, he moved out and never looked back. Until now, that was. Sitting in David's office, waiting for the man himself to appear, all he had were memories of his own father at the forefront of his mind. Weirdly it wasn't the horrible memories either. It was the man he had been before his wife took her life. Kind, gentle, loving. Sitting there now, waiting for David, Jim realised he actually *missed* his father. Another thought: Maybe this was what it would take to get them back together? Maybe once this conversation was done, he'd call his own dad? Not to ask permission, but to tell him he was getting married and that - if he wanted to - there was an invitation with his name on it. Maybe he'd come? Better yet, maybe he was sober now too? It had been long enough for him to get the help he had clearly needed.

Just as Jim's mind started to drift again, this time to darker thoughts wondering whether his dad was even still alive, the office door opened and David walked in. The suddenness with which he burst into the room startled Jim and his heart skipped a beat. Once it regained its natural rhythm, it started to race as he shifted his focus to mentally prepare himself to ask the question.

'Sorry to keep you waiting,' David said. He walked around to the other side of his large oak desk and took a seat. 'One of those days,' he explained.

'It's fine,' Jim said. 'I'm sorry for just dropping in unannounced like this.'

'Not a problem. It's good to see you.'

Jim couldn't help but wonder whether the sentiment would remain the same once he'd asked the question, or whether he would - at last - see the disappointment in David's eyes which he'd been expecting ever since first being introduced.

'So how have you been?' David asked, killing the immediate silence which fell between the two of them.

'I'm good,' Jim said as he struggled to get the "other" words out.

'That's good.'

On the drive over, once he'd dropped Mitch off, Jim had gone over in his head what he would say and, how he would say it. By the time he pulled up onto the driveway, he had the whole spiel ready to go. By the time he knocked on the door - and the maid opened it - *everything* had been forgotten.

'And yourself?'

David laughed. 'I'm well, thank you.'

Just as before, a silence fell between them once more.

'Scary, isn't it?' David got up from his chair and went to a drinks cabinet along the far wall. He poured himself a scotch and, then, he poured a second one for Jim. He took the two drinks back to his desk and handed one to Jim before taking his chair for a second time.

'What is?' Jim asked.

'I remember when I asked my father-in-law. I was terrified. He was this overbearing man and… In fact to this day I don't think I've seen him smile. Can you imagine sitting opposite someone who just had one expression on their face and that expression was "stern"?' David laughed as an old memory played through for him. 'Well I'm not the same as him and I can see you're struggling so, to put you out of your misery, the answer is "yes".'

'The answer?'

'You want to marry my daughter.'

Jim stuttered like a fool, unsure what to say as David just laughed again. 'How did you know?'

'Well Laura's at work and, when you knocked on the door, you didn't even ask to see her. You asked to see me. Now as much as I love your company, you haven't popped round to just see me before so, it stood to reason that you were here to ask for my daughter's hand in marriage. Either that or you were here to try and blackmail me…' He laughed.

'Blackmail you?'

'We've had it before. One of her exes thought he had some dirt on me which he was threatening to sell to the tabloids if I didn't give him a pay out.' David laughed again. It was a long time ago but something he'd never been able to forget, given how ridiculous the situation had been. Not least of all because there was no truth in what he was being threatened with. Laura's ex had misheard a conversation and put two and two together to come up with five. David's smile disappeared from his face. 'You're not here to blackmail me, are you?'

'No! I wanted to ask if I could marry your daughter.'

'Ah good. So I was right. Would have been a shame if we would have had to kill you too,' he said in a very matter of fact tone. He paused for just a couple of seconds and then started to laugh again. 'We didn't have him killed. Only beaten. It's all good.' Then, with a serious face, he asked, 'Still want to marry my daughter?'

'I do.'

Had this been the first conversation they'd had, Jim might have been a little concerned about how this was playing out but - he knew David had a somewhat dark sense of humour, thanks to previous conversations. One example, in the middle of dinner, David had suddenly come out with one of the darkest jokes Jim had ever heard. He literally blurted it out, in the middle of an otherwise "normal" conversation. Jim had been the only one to really laugh but only because of the shock he was in. It was just a shame he couldn't recall the joke.

'Thought about how you're going to ask yet?'

'No. I just know that I want to ask.' Jim reached into his pocket and pulled out the ring-box. He put the box on the desk and slid it towards David. 'I did get this today though.'

David picked the box up. He didn't immediately open it. Instead, he asked, 'May I?'

'Please.'

David opened the box and revealed the ring within. He smiled. 'Must be pretty confident she'll say yes. Doesn't look cheap.'

Without thinking, Jim said, 'It's fine - the lady in the shop said I have a few weeks to return it...'

David looked at him blankly for a moment, unsure whether he was joking or not. After what felt like a lifetime to Jim, who realised he'd fucked up by saying that, David said, 'Shame you didn't wait a little while before buying it. You really want to make a good impression and get a yes from her? You should propose at Halloween...'

'Halloween?'

David laughed. 'Her favourite time of the year...'

BOY

NEARLY

PROPOSES TO GIRL

5

Despite the burning desire to ask Laura to marry him, Jim refrained from doing so. As per his would-be father-in-laws advice, he pocketed the ring with the plan to pop the question on Halloween. *Her favourite day,* according to her father yet, in the run-up to the event, Jim couldn't help but wonder whether he'd been telling the truth, or just stalling Jim from popping the question. The reason for the doubt was Laura's changing mood.

Throughout September she'd been fine. She seemed happy in herself and, she seemed happy spending her free time with Jim too. But, as October continued, Jim couldn't help but feel as though something was wrong. Laura wasn't laughing as much as she used to, nor was she joking around with him. Everything she said was "to the point" and, even a little cold at times. Jim didn't want to be *that* guy, always seeking reassurance that things were great between them but, at the same time, he knew he couldn't just stand there and say nothing. After all, if there *was* something up then there might be a chance to fix it. If he said nothing and continued to let whatever it was fester away, then it could go past the point of no return and - before he knew it - he'd be single again. Single and past the period of return for the ring he'd hidden away back at his apartment.

Laura and Jim were in a pop-up Halloween store at the edge of the city. Every year, at the end of September, this store would take over a space often used for art shows and such. It would always sell a massive collection of Halloween decorations - priced from just a couple of quid up to the more elaborate animatronic ghouls which cost hundreds. A popular store, it would always be heaving with customers looking to dress up themselves, or their houses come October 31st and, then, by November 2nd, it was gone for another year.

Laura was going through the displays with a face like thunder. Jim was a few feet away, watching her discreetly. She'd barely spoken all day and, not for the first time, Jim was wondering whether he'd said something which had pissed her off. He wasn't entirely sure because, usually, she was pretty quick to say if something was upsetting her. Usually. Now, and not for the first time, she was quiet. She went from display to display with a dark aura about her person, which made Jim feel uncomfortable. He wasn't the only one to notice this either. Other people seemed to take note of her mood, despite her saying nothing to them. When she walked close to these people, they instinctively moved away.

Even though Jim was all too familiar with the old saying "let sleeping dogs lie", he couldn't ignore her mood anymore. He walked over to where she was thumbing through a catalogue of mail order outfits and, in a quiet voice, asked, 'Are you okay?'

'What are you talking about?' she snapped, seemingly surprised by his question.

'You seem… I don't know… I seem off.'

'Off?'

'Yeah. Not yourself. Like I've pissed you off or something.' Unsure whether he really wanted the answer, he asked, 'Have I pissed you off?'

'What? No. It's just… Well look around you.'

Unsure what she was talking about, Jim looked around the store. People were milling around, minding their own business. Other than that, there wasn't really much to notice. 'What?'

'That for a start,' she said as she pointed across the shop.

Jim followed her finger's pointing and noticed Christmas decorations hanging at the far end of the store. Every year Christmas seemed to be getting earlier and earlier but, he didn't see any issues. 'I don't get it,' he said, confused.

'We haven't even had Halloween yet and here they are, ramming Christmas down our throats. They never used to do that here but, for some reason, now it's *normal*. It just pisses me off. Come Christmas they'll be selling Easter eggs and so on.'

Jim still didn't understand how this was enough to poison her mood. But, he also wasn't stupid enough to question it. Thankfully, he didn't have to.

'And what is going on with the weather?' She continued, 'We're supposed to be going around with warm cups of hot chocolate with lumps of marshmallow in it, getting excited about Halloween and yet...' She gestured to what she was wearing - shorts and a tee shirt. 'I feel like I should be going to the beach...'

'Well, I mean, you look great...'

'Thank you but that's not the point. Everything just feels off at the moment and it has done for a while now.'

'I'm sorry.'

'It's not your fault! You have nothing to be sorry for...'

'But I am sorry that you're feeling this way. I see Christmas decorations and don't really think of anything. I think it's because I don't really *see* them, you know? Like, they don't register. Well, not until closer to the time.' He continued, 'And the weather... I guess I've not been helping by saying how nice it is, have I?' Jim wasn't the only one commenting on the weather though. It was a very "British" thing to do, wasn't it? In August, when the heavens opened, people moaned daily about it. In September and October, with the nicer weather, they praised it. Until this moment, he never stopped to think there'd be some people out there who wouldn't be happy to see this kind of weather come in. In truth, he still didn't understand why the weather would be an issue. Again, he wasn't stupid enough to question this.

'Come on,' Laura said, 'I'll do this another day. I'm not really in the mood.'

Before Jim could convince her otherwise, Laura put her shopping basket down and started towards the exit. Jim followed, unsure as to how he could even start to make any of this better for Laura. He was also questioning - in his head - whether that really was "it" or whether there was something else bothering her. Something more serious, which would explain the over reaction to a few Christmas decorations and the sunshine.

Outside, the sun shone down in their faces and as they made their way to Jim's car, he instinctively reached for his sunglasses. He only stopped himself from putting them on when he realised it *could* have upset Laura further. A reminder that it was unseasonably bright and cheerful still, despite Halloween fast approaching.

6

'I'm sorry I'm being a bitch,' Laura said as Jim drove her back to her home. 'It's just…' She hesitated a moment. Jim glanced over to her, to see what was wrong. From her expression, it was clear she was searching for a better explanation as to why her mood was off. 'When you were growing up, do you remember the Christmas days when it snowed?'

'Sure.' In England, especially in the city where it was a few degrees warmer, snow days were rare. At least, snow days where the snow actually laid.

'You would be indoors. The Christmas lights would be on, the smell of dinner cooking in the kitchen would be in the air, along with the smell of pines from the tree… It would be early in the morning and your dad would already be drinking, as would your mum who'd be downing the champagne in...' Laura stopped mid-sentence as she realised what she was saying. Jim's mother was dead and his father was an alcoholic. 'Shit, I'm sorry. I didn't mean...'

Jim gave her a reassuring smile. 'It's fine. I know what you mean. You're talking about a perfect Christmas. Inside is warm, you've everything you want and outside, the snow just paints the scenery into something postcard-perfect, yeah?'

'Yes. Like the snow makes it all that more magical, even if you don't go out in it. It just makes it Christmassy!'

'So what you're saying is, Halloween won't feel like Halloween if it's sunny?'

'We haven't spoken about Halloween yet but it's my favourite time of the year. The whole street comes out to celebrate with a street party. We huddle around fire pits in each of the gardens, we toast marshmallows, there are candy buckets for the kids, we bob for apples... Everyone gets involved and makes an effort and... At this rate I'm worried people will be firing up the barbecues and setting aside the costumes! It won't be the same...'

'Maybe the weather will turn by then?'

'I already looked. It's meant to be warm right the way through,' Laura said with a disappointed tone in her voice. Jim didn't know what to say. What he did know was, if Halloween wasn't perfect for her then he couldn't propose. Unless, he wondered, maybe such a gesture would *fix* things for her? It was a big gamble.

'What is it?' Laura asked him, sensing a change in his own mood.

Thinking quick on his feet, Jim said, 'I just feel bad for you. I wish I could make it how you like it, if that makes sense.'

'It does.'

'Although,' Jim thought out loud, if only to change the subject slightly, 'how do you think people who live abroad feel?'

'What do you mean?'

'People who live in hotter climates? Surely their Halloween is always warm, right? How do you think they feel come the night?'

'They're used to warmer weather. For them, bad weather would ruin the holiday because it's not what they used to…'

'Ah,' Jim said. That made sense. 'Maybe we should book someplace cold to go for Halloween? Get away from…'

'No!' Laura explained, 'I'm *always* home for Halloween.' Then, to save face, she continued, 'I'm sure it will be fine. I'm just being stupid.' She forced a smile for Jim. He could tell it was being *forced*. Still, he smiled back as his mind started to question whether she'd be impressed with a Christmas proposal instead. With the Halloween one hanging in the balance, he needed a back-up plan after all.

'Thank you for running me into town,' Laura said as Jim pulled his car up onto her driveway.

'My pleasure…'

Laura laughed. 'It wasn't really though, was it?'

'It's fine. I'm just sorry you're not feeling too happy about things at the moment. I wish I could make it all better for you,' Jim said. He was still battling with himself about proposing to her. He was desperate to do it, and to hear her say "yes" but at the same time, he wanted it to be done *right*. And proposing just to cheer her day up was not what he'd originally had in mind.

'I'll be okay,' she said. 'I guess I just woke up in a funny mood. I'm sure tomorrow will be better.'

Jim smiled. 'Especially if the temperature drops and it starts to rain.'

Laura smiled. 'Temperature, yes. But let's keep the rain away, yeah?'

'Good job you said that. I was about to go home and do a rain dance for you.'

'Aw, you'd do that for me?' Laura said sarcastically. 'Listen, I know we haven't really talked about Halloween before but… Like I said, we do this big *thing* on the street. All the neighbours come out and get together… It's fun…'

'Yeah, you were saying,' Jim said. He was expecting the next sentence to be along the lines of, she couldn't see him on Halloween because she was busy. But...

'Would you like to join us? I think you'd get a kick out of it.'

'Are you kidding? Of course, I'd like to come.'

Laura smiled. It looked like a weight had been lifted from her shoulders. Jim couldn't help but wonder, was she really worried about him saying "no"? Perhaps he wasn't the only one in the relationship to be a little lower in confidence than a "normal" person. 'That's great,' she said, beaming.

And who knows, Jim thought*, if the night is that good - he could still propose to her...* He smiled. 'Thank you for asking.'

'Call you tonight?'

Jim nodded. 'Whenever you're ready.'

'Great!' Laura leaned over to where Jim was sitting and gave him a tender kiss on the cheek. 'Talk to you tonight.' And, with that, she got out of the car. Jim just sat there, in the driver's seat, watching her via the rearview mirror as she made her way up towards the house. He smiled to himself. At least she seemed happier now and, hopefully, she'd be even happier in a couple of weeks, if he proposed. His heart skipped a beat at the mere thought of it and he chuckled to himself. 'Get it out of your system now… *Get it out of your system now…*' The last thing he wanted to do was to get nervous and stumble over his lines, *when* the time came. If she was to say "yes", his fluffing up his grand speech would be something that would haunt him for the rest of their lives together. He could picture it now, their grandchildren asking how they met and Laura teasing him for spluttering over what he wanted to say. 'Fuck that,' he mumbled to himself as, slowly, he pulled away from the driveway.

GIRL FUCKS BOY

7

Jim woke up to the sound of laughter. As the room slowly came into focus, he realised the laughing wasn't the same as a "normal" person's laugh but, rather, more Hyena like. Through a thumping headache he also realised that it wasn't playing out "live" either. It was pre-recorded, playing over and over on a seemingly never-ending loop.

With slurred speech, almost as if he had been drinking, he shouted, 'Shut up!' The noise didn't stop though. It just continued going round and around and around - that never ending loop.

Jim sat up on the rickety old bed, planted centre in the otherwise bare room which he didn't recognise. He frowned, unsure as to how he had got there. Or even where "there" was. He looked around, trying to make sense of everything but making none. The floorboards were bare and looked almost rotten in their appearance. The walls were bare too, with the exception of a few strips of ripped wallpaper and patches of damp. The windows were boarded up, allowing only a slither of light to penetrate into the near dark room. The bed he'd been laying on, nothing more than a filthy mattress stained with God only knew what.

Across from him, there was a closed door on the far wall. A keyhole in the handle let a little more light spill in from whatever room was beyond (he presumed a hallway). Wherever he was, Jim had no idea how he had got there. With the laughter playing loudly on the speakers still, he knew he didn't want to stay there any longer than necessary. He pulled himself up off the bed and swayed there a moment as the room spun around him, unsure whether he was going to vomit up his stomach's contents. A flashed memory popped to mind for just a split second; he'd been eating a hotdog. If he was to throw up now, *that* was what would be coming up. It wasn't much of a memory but, it was better than nothing and - thankfully - triggered more...

BEFORE

'There's no need to be nervous,' Laura said, reassuring Jim as they approached a group of her neighbours.

'That's easy for you to say. You know everyone.'

It was Halloween. The sun had gone done and, as they did every year at this time, the neighbours had all come out and gathered at the end of the street, close to a derelict house. Jim could see they'd set up big screens, shelters for if it suddenly rained (not that it was due to), more than a few fire-pits and BBQ stands. Close to those, there were a few tables - on top of which there were drinks, rolls, crisps and chocolates.

'Jesus. You weren't joking, were you? You guys really do go all out for Halloween.'

Laura laughed. 'I told you! It's fun. Come on,' she said as she quickened her pace, 'I'll introduce you.'

Jim noticed another group approaching from the other side of the road. Dressed as ghouls, the couple also had what looked like a bag of drinks with them.

'I feel like I should have brought something with me.'

'You brought yourself. That's enough,' Laura said. As they neared, she called out to one of the men, 'Murray!' At the sound of his name being called, an elderly man turned to see Laura approaching. He grinned at the sight of her and walked over.

'Laura. I was starting to think you weren't coming…'

'Miss this? Never.'

'And I see you brought a friend,' Murray said. He looked Jim up and down and his grin widened. 'He'll do,' he said. Jim frowned, unsure what he meant. 'Murray. I live next door to Laura. Pleased to meet you.'

Jim smiled and shook the hand Murray extended. 'I'm Jim. I don't live next door to Laura,' he said in a failed effort to be funny. Jim noticed another group approaching the congregation. Just as the other couple had a bag of goodies with them, so too did this group. Jim explained again, 'I'm sorry, I didn't bring anything... I didn't know that was a thing...'

Murray smiled. 'Not a problem. You brought yourself! That's enough! Here, come with me... I'll get you a drink.' With a hand on Jim's shoulder, Murray marched him towards a table of drinks. Laura smiled, happy that Murray seemed to like Jim as much as her own family did.

Wobbly on his legs, Jim walked over to the only door in the room. With a nervous hand, he took a hold of the handle and gave it a twist. The moment he pulled the door open, the recording of the laughter immediately stopped. Such was the suddenness, Jim stopped in his tracks - unsure as to whether something else was going to happen. For a moment, he stood there motionless. Beyond the crumbling walls of the building, he could hear music playing as though people were having a party nearby. Really straining, he could hear laughter. Real, human laughter.

In front of him, at the other end of the landing space, there was a window. Just as the bedroom one had been boarded, so too had this one. Only a few slithers of light spilled onto the dark landing, through a couple of narrow slits. Slits that he could see out of…

Jim walked over to the window and squinted through one of the narrow gaps. More confusion hit home when his suspicions were confirmed: He was in the derelict house at the end of Laura's street. But why? He banged on the wooden boards and shouted through, 'Hello? This some kind of prank? Well very funny, you got me!' No one looked up to the window. Down on the ground, they all seemed preoccupied. Jim repositioned himself so that he could see through to what they were looking at. All of them were watching the brightly lit screen standing tall in the garden.

Jim called through again, 'Hello?! You guys going to tell me what's going on?!' Still, no one looked up to the window. Instead, it looked like they were laughing. Then, they were pointing to the screen, like something had happened. 'Hello?!' Jim wasn't aware that, behind him, a figure was standing in the doorway he'd not long since come from. Quietly, it took a step towards Jim.

The screen played what was happening inside the house to those waiting outside, thanks to hidden cameras - filming in night vision - dotted around the property. The entire street had come out to see the *rat* run the *maze*, just as they did every year, and most had placed bets for how long said rat would survive.

Murray was standing at the front of the group, along with Dave and Laura. All three of them were staring up at the screen. None of them saying anything as *The Clown* stepped closer still to an oblivious Jim. As tension continued to rise, Murray took a bite of his hotdog.

'Needs mustard,' he said. He turned his back on the screen and walked back over to the table, where the condiments had been left. 'Evening, Bob.' Bob was standing by the table, trying to decide what to put on his burger.

'Evening, Murray. Good turn out again, huh?'

'Sure is.'

8

One last ditch attempt. Jim banged on the board covering the window and screamed out, 'Hello? Can you hear me?' As far as he was aware, no one was paying him any attention. In truth, most of them were glued to the screen showing Jim. Frustrated and confused, he took a step back from the window when, behind him, a floorboard creaked under the weight of the other person's heavy foot. Jim spun on the spot and jumped back in shock at the sight of a heavy-set man made up to look like a clown.

Before Jim could admit to the stranger scaring the shit out of him, the clown grinned and grabbed either side of Jim's head with his gloved hands. Immediately he started to apply pressure. Jim screamed out loud as he started pulling at the man's wrists, desperate to yank him away. The clown - more beast than man - laughed at Jim's pathetic attempts to break free. His laughter increased at the sound of a "crack"; a small fracture in the back of the skull. Then, with a grunt and display of sheer power, he lifted Jim clean off the floor by his head. Jim's screams continued as he frantically kicked against the clown, not that his flurry of kicks helped to get him free, and - still - he clawed and pulled at the beast's wrists and-

The clown twisted Jim's head in a quick motion. His neck sounded off with a god-awful crack before Jim's body went limp. Outside, the watching crowd fell silent.

'Well… *fuck*…' Murray said. He took his betting slip from his jacket pocket and screwed it into a ball. 'I really thought I had it this year…'

Bob did the same. He turned to Laura and pointed out, 'I think you found the runt of the litter this year.'

Laura didn't say anything. She was just staring up at the screen. The clown was still holding Jim up by his head. He pressed his thumbs against Jim's eyes and started to push into them. The screen's heavy-duty speakers played out the unpleasant squelching noises as Jim's once-seeing eyes turned to mush. A few more moments watching, and Laura muttered, 'With all he's been through in life, I honestly thought he would have been more of a fighter.'

David put his arm around her. 'I'm sorry, baby. If it's any consolation, I thought he was going to go further as well.'

'He barely got out of the room.'

'Just wasn't a fighter, I guess.' David glanced over towards the fire pit and asked, 'Want to toast some marshmallows?'

'I'd like that.'

David smiled and, arm still around his daughter's shoulders, together they walked towards the closest fire pit.

'Wasn't expecting that,' said Katy.

Katy was Bob's wife. Together, they had a daughter called Erin. As a family, they were always trying to keep up with their neighbours. If someone on the street got a new car, so did Katy and Bob. If someone applied for an extension, or similar, then they did too. It hadn't gone unnoticed by the other neighbours either, who had joked about it over the years, but - at the same time - it was also pretty irritating. Living next to them, you were never given time to enjoy a new purchase without them knocking on the door to show that they'd got something new too. Even on Halloween, their constant one-upmanship was evident.

'You should see our daughter's candidate. For the first time ever, I actually placed a bet that they'll make it out of the house.'

'That's pretty confident,' David said, trying his hardest not to roll his eyes.

'Honestly I looked at…' She paused a moment as she tried to recall Laura's boyfriend's name.

'Jim,' Laura said, helpfully.

'Yes. Him. I looked at him and knew he wasn't going to get very far. Obviously came from weak stock. Did you know, our man used to play football for the county? Would have gone pro too, had it not been for a scandal he was involved in a few years back.'

David just smiled. 'In our family, we try and avoid scandal.'

'Of course. As you should. A man of your standing. Thankfully, in the creative world, my husband's work only increases if we are found to be embroiled in some kind of scandal. Not sure how that works or why only *some* of the guilty ever get cancelled but hey ho… Anyway, I hope you've put a bet on him. If you haven't, you might want to rectify that before the proceedings start. Wouldn't want you to regret anything.'

As of this moment, there was only one thing David was regretting and it wasn't his lack of bet, or his daughter's poor choice of "man". It was the fact he'd chosen to come to *this* particular fire pit. Of course Katy was going to want to talk crap and brag about "whatever". David really should have expected it by now. As she continued to waffle with words unheard, David couldn't help but wonder whether he'd get away with locking *her* in the funhouse. A quick glance over to Bob and it was clear Bob was making a clear effort to avoid his wife by talking to anyone and everyone else. *Poor bastard*, David thought. *Imagine being married to this.*

A merciful distraction and excuse to leave Katy ranting by the fire; the front door of the house opened. Everyone looked over as the clown threw Jim's lifeless body out onto the grass. No sooner had the body landed, the clown stepped back into the building and slammed the door shut. Slowly, some of the men in the group started towards where the body lay. The clown had played his part. Now it was turn for them to play their part and, for them, that involved "clean up" duties.

As the first of the men approached, his eyes were immediately drawn to a small box which had fallen from Jim's pocket. He called back over his shoulder, 'David? Might want to see this.'

GIRL LIKES GIRL

9

With time to kill before the next *contribution*, Laura walked into her bedroom with the small ring-box in hand. Without a word, she walked over to the top drawer in her chest of drawers and pulled it open. Inside, there were a number of boxes, similar to the one she had in her hand. Before adding it to her impressive collection, she opened it and looked at the ring inside. It was pretty, sure enough. It wasn't the prettiest though. Still, she smiled at his thought and closed the box lid. Then, she quietly put the ring-box into the drawer with the others. If her memory served correctly, this was her tenth one now, not that she'd ever got to hear the actual proposals being made. Her dad was clever in the way he stopped the potential husbands from asking the question too early, pointing out that her favourite day of the year was Halloween. If they didn't take the not-so subtle hint he put down before them, he would often take it further by saying she'd always dreamed of being proposed to on *that* day. Whilst some were confused by this - it was an evening associated with things that went bump in the night after all - none of them questioned what he said. Why would they? Being her father, he would want what was best for his daughter and if he didn't want them to marry her then - he simply wouldn't have given his blessing. Knowing they were only in his daughter's life for the event, David never turned any of them down. Even if he, and the rest of the family, hated who Laura had snared, they always played nice to ensure they had a competitor for the evening.

 Laura stood a moment and looked at the various jewellery boxes in front of her. Each one represented a life lost. Each one represented a missed opportunity to hear someone ask her to marry them. Laura didn't know how she felt about missing out on hearing the questions. Some of the men were so far from her typical "type" that she wasn't even sure she'd be able to keep a straight face, if they had asked. And laughing in the face of someone proposing? Never a good look. Also, if they did manage to get the question out, would it make it harder to put them into the competition? Would there be an additional bond there which - suddenly - she wouldn't want to break? It hadn't happened yet but, if it did, she wasn't sure what the rest of the street would say. If she met someone who was meant to be a part of their games, would they let her change her mind if she decided not to put them in? Or would they insist. The deal was done and it wasn't up to any of them to break it. At least, not without consequences. Laura tried to push the thoughts from her head and, she closed the drawer shut.

'Another ring?' Erin's voice came from Laura's bedroom doorway. Having not heard Erin approach, Laura couldn't help but to jump when Erin spoke to her. She turned to face her and nodded. 'You must really play your part in making them believe they love you,' Erin said. 'Too much hassle for me,' she continued as she ran her dainty hand through her long blonde hair.

'It saves them getting bored and running off,' Laura said in her defence. That had happened one year, when her heart wasn't really in it. As much as she loved watching the giant screens, she questioned why it was down to the daughters to bring in the players. They were having to con people into coming down, they were having to spend time with people they wouldn't normally go near and what did the parents do? The parents bought the food and drinks and set the play-list for the music. It was hardly the same as what the daughters were having to put themselves through.

That year - when Laura was questioning everything - her "boyfriend" at the time got bored and broke it off a week before Halloween. David was fuming with her, as were the neighbours and other town officials. There was a quota to be met and, she'd potentially ruined it for *everyone*. Had it not been for the fact one of the daughters had managed to pull some twins, everything could have changed that night.

'You want to stop them getting bored? That's easy,' Erin said with a cheeky smile. 'Just lie on your back and open your legs. That's all I do.' It wasn't quite all that

Erin did. She also went on top, swallowed their load and let them fuck her in the arse too. She also kept them hanging on with the promise of having a "fit friend" who wanted to join them too. With the filthiest sex "on tap", the "boyfriends" very rarely got bored. Even if they did, and they went off and fucked someone else, they still came back, simply because they *could*.

'What about him? What was the sex like with him?' Erin asked, a cheeky smile on her face. It was the same every year. She always wanted all the dirty little details. On the times Laura - or any of the other girls - felt like sharing, she would instantly share what "her man" was like in bed. Nine times out of ten she'd report back that he was a "stud" and fucked her raw. Whether that was the truth or not, no one knew for sure. Some of the girls just presumed it was wishful thinking and others just guessed she'd picked up this habit of embellishing from her mother, Katy.

Not in the mood, Laura simply said, 'It was okay.'

'Sounds boring then,' Erin said with a giggle. She sat on the edge of the bed. 'You should have seen my guy. He'd go down on me without even being asked. And he had this thing he did with his tongue…'

'I don't really want to know,' Laura said. She walked over and perched herself down next to Erin.

'I thought you might like to know this one,' Erin laughed. 'I got him to teach me…' She leaned forward and kissed Laura on the lips. She pulled away momentarily, with a smile on her face, and said, 'Yummy…' Then, 'I've missed you…'

Laura blushed. 'I missed you too.'

'Less talking,' Erin said. She pushed her friend back on the bed and moved down so that her face was between Laura's legs. With a dirty grin on her face, and a wicked glint in her eyes, she lifted Laura's black skirt out of the way.

Laura closed her eyes and let out a soft sigh as she felt Erin kiss her pussy, through her already-wet panties. She'd hoped Erin was going to follow her up to her room, when she brought the ring in. After months of avoiding one another, as they worked on their contributions to the evening's events, they both craved one another's touch and, as a result, neither could wait for morning.

Erin pulled Laura's panties to one side and, without hesitation, she pushed her tongue inside her neat, moist slit.

'Oh shit!' Laura gasped as Erin's tongue proceeded to fuck her. Despite knowing they didn't have as much time as either of them wanted, before they'd be missed by their oblivious parents, Laura bit her bottom lip before she begged, 'Don't stop. Don't you stop…'

Erin had no intention of stopping until she'd taste Laura's sweet cum coating her tongue. As she continued orally pleasuring her secret girlfriend, she reached down between her legs and rubbed herself through her leggings.

10

'Where have you been?' David called out as Laura returned back to the street party. So as not to arouse suspicion, she went back alone whilst Erin hung back.

'I put the ring away as I didn't want to lose it.'

'Surprised you bothered,' David said. 'Not exactly anything to write home about, was it?'

'Oh I don't know. I liked it.'

David held out a glass of champagne towards Laura. She took it with a smile and, the two of them clinked their glasses together.

'They're about to put the next one in,' David said.

'Whose is this one?'

'Erin's guy. Hopefully he'll roll off the bed and break his neck, or something just as stupid.' David was only saying that because, at this point, it was the only way they were going to save face with Jim's poor performance.

Jim had been the second of the competitors to enter the house that night. The first had been a young lad called Ben. Ben had got further than Jim, pushing the clown back into the main bedroom and then bolting the door locked. He had ultimately met his ending when he opened the wrong door and had a shotgun blast his head off. It was a simple trap: gun attached to the wall at head height, string going from trigger to door-handle. Twist the handle and the string pulls back, activating the trigger. If you don't know the gun is hanging there, it is a quick and unseen death. With the way the heads pop and brain, blood and skull fragments splash the surrounds, it's a messy one too. It is also a great crowd-pleaser but, for the sake of keeping things interesting, there's only ever one bullet loaded into the gun. That way, when the next person goes in, they don't die in the same manner.

Laura knew her father was less than impressed with Jim's escape attempt and, she blamed herself. As had already been pointed out, she'd picked a dud. But then, unlike the others, she only wanted to pick those who weren't as lucky in life as others. She wanted the weaker of the species because, in a fucked up way, she figured she was doing them a favour. Not only do they feel loved for a few months, prior to Halloween, but then she sees to it that they're put out of their misery. She *was* doing them a favour.

'I'm sorry about Jim,' Laura said. 'I thought he would do better.'

'At the end of the day, it's disappointing for us only. He still served his purpose, didn't he?'

'He did.'

'So then,' David said with a kind smile, 'there's nothing to be sorry for, is there?'

'I guess not.' Happy that her dad seemed understanding, Laura asked, 'Did you place a bet on the next one?'

'I didn't want to give Katy and Bob the satisfaction,' David said. At the end of the evening, they couldn't afford any of the competitors to escape. They had a quota to reach and so, all those who entered needed their bloodshed within the crumbling walls. That didn't mean they wanted their family's contribution to perish fastest though. They wanted to have been seen to bring forward the strongest candidate. No one wins prizes for coming last.

'You ready to see a real man in action?' Erin's voice came from behind and - for the second time that night - made Laura jump.

As Erin approached, David made his excuses, 'I'll leave you two to it.'

David walked off just as Erin reached Laura. She smiled sweetly at her and quietly said, 'I hope you know, I've just masturbated on your bed. Sorry if it's a little damp when you get into it tonight.'

Laura laughed as her face immediately flushed red. 'Ssh!'

Erin changed the subject, 'I'm going to grab myself a drink. Care to accompany me to the screen?'

Laura nodded. 'Sure.' As she followed Erin over to where Murray was pouring out some more drinks, she asked, 'What's his name anyway?'

BOY FUCKS GIRL

11

BEFORE

'DUNCAN! FUCK ME! HARDER!' Erin was on Duncan's bed, kneeling on hands and knees. Duncan was standing on the floor behind her, a naked mess of sweat and fat as he barebacked Erin.

With her eyes closed up tight, she was imagining Brad Pitt standing behind her, fucking her cunt whilst she reached between her legs and rubbed herself. Whilst Duncan wasn't bad to look at, it was safe to say he was no Brad Pitt and, with his lack of interest in foreplay, Erin needed a more God-like figure in her mind if she wanted to be wet enough for a comfortable fuck.

'FUCK ME!' Erin screamed again, safe in the knowledge that he lived alone and there was no one to disturb with her cries. But, that aside, her demand was met with Duncan slowing his pace until he stopped completely. He was breathing heavy; almost gasping. Erin glanced over her shoulder, back at him. Surprised he'd stopped, she asked, 'Did you cum?' She got her answer when he pulled out and she felt a dribble of his spunk run out down over her pussy. She pulled a face. 'Ergh. That's a yes then.' She moved onto the other side of the bed and laid out flat before reaching for her rucksack, which was on the floor nearby.

Duncan laid down next to her and tried to catch his breath. 'That was great,' he said, more enthused than she was. 'I needed that…' He turned to Erin and smiled at her so as to show his appreciation. His smile promptly disappeared when he noticed she'd pulled a vibrator from her bag and was buzzing it against her clitoris. 'What the fuck?'

'Just because you're finished,' Erin said pointedly, 'it doesn't mean I have…'

'Well I can help…'

Despite the pleasurable sensations of the toy teasing her clitoris, Erin couldn't help but to laugh. They'd been fucking for a couple of minutes at most, with zero foreplay, and *now* he reckoned he could pleasure her? 'I'm good,' she said. Her eyes were still closed and - in her head - Brad was holding the toy for her, as she just laid there and *let him*. Her imagined scenario was momentarily stopped when Duncan pulled the toy away from her.

'What are you doing?' she asked, grumpily.

Duncan winked at her, 'Trust me. I'm good with my tongue…'

She was about to protest when, with no warning, she felt the warmth of his tongue press against her aching pussy. Erin sighed in pleasure. Even if he couldn't take her all the way, she figured, she'd let him try for a minute or two. It seemed like the polite thing to do, given his eagerness to help her reach her owed climax. A few moments later and, she felt the tip of his thumb press against her clitoris. Surprised with his level of multi-tasking, a little gasp of pleasure slipped from her mouth.

Duncan and Erin were laying on the bed. He was staring up at the ceiling and, as was often the case after they'd fucked, she was surfing her social media accounts on her phone. With Halloween fast approaching, she was already lining up a "date" for the following year, not that Duncan knew. If he did happen to look at her phone and see another guy's message, she'd just say it was a "friend". After all, they didn't know each other well enough yet for him to know who she was friends with.

Bored with the lack of conversation, Duncan rolled onto his side and watched Erin for a while. Aware she had an audience, Erin was quick to close her messages down and revert back to aimlessly scrolling the pages of negativity which Facebook usually brought with it.

'Anything interesting?' Duncan asked.

'Same old, same old,' Erin said. She was actually genuinely surprised he hadn't fallen asleep already. That was normally what happened once he shot his load.

He'd fall asleep, she'd surf the net for a while and then either doze off too, or creep out and go home. With nothing of worth to really see, she closed her phone and set it to the side, on the bedside cabinet.

'Oh I forgot to say,' Duncan continued, 'but we've been invited out on Halloween. A few friends of mine are having a party. Could be a laugh, if you're interested?'

Unsure of what to say immediately, Erin just smiled whilst she processed what he'd said. *A party?* That was the problem with picking a popular boy. They were normally invited to all the parties and, from experience, it was usually hard to convince them to dump their friends.

Still stalling, Erin said, 'A party?'

Duncan nodded. 'Good bunch of people. It'll be a laugh…' He asked, 'What do you think? Up for being my plus one?' Erin scrunched her face up. It was enough for Duncan to know there was a problem. 'That's a no then…'

'I've kind of already promised to be somewhere,' she said.

'It's fine. We can just...'

Before he finished his sentence, Erin continued, 'I've promised *we'll* be somewhere...'

'Me? I told my friends that I'd be going...'

'What if I said my friends would be at the party we've been invited to?'

'I would say, I would hope so... Seeing as they invited you to a party. Be a bit weird for them not to be there if they asked you to go.'

Erin continued, 'What if I told you my friends would be *really grateful* if you came to the party with me?' She waited for the penny to drop. It didn't take long. 'You see what I'm saying?'

'So this party we're going to? Where is it?'

Murray handed Duncan a drink. He reiterated, 'Yep, every year.' He added, 'I don't think a single person from this street has missed it since we started it in fact. How's that for dedication and community spirit?'

'That's pretty insane,' Duncan said. 'Had I known it was a street party, I would have told my friends to come too.'

'Maybe they can come next year,' Murray said. He took a swig from his drink in the hope Duncan would do the same.

Erin chipped in, 'I'm sure I can invite them next year.' She smiled innocently. Murray laughed at her comment as he knew the true meaning behind it. Duncan laughed just because.

Erin was standing outside with Duncan. With Murray, the three of them were standing by the drinks table. Duncan spotted something over by the derelict-looking house. He said, 'Don't worry… My friends can hold their drink better than that guy anyway.' He pointed to a man - seemingly unconscious - being carried towards the house.

'Excitement of the evening just gets to some people,' Murray said.

Duncan's attention had already turned to the giant screen. 'So what films are we seeing tonight? Hopefully the old classics from the 80s... Love me some of those old films. They're crap yet, somehow... Brilliant. That even make sense?'

'They'll be starting soon enough,' Murray said. 'Drink up. Plenty more from where that came from.'

Duncan laughed. He said to Erin, 'Clearly going to be a fun party.'

Erin smiled. 'Definitely.'

BOY FUCKS BOY

12

Duncan tumbled down the stairs, yelling out with each step hit. At his tangled body bumped to the ground floor, his ankle twisted awkwardly and the bone beneath the skin cracked through. His yell turned to a scream of agony as he instinctively reached for his broken ankle. From the top of the stairs, the clown laughed but - that was all he did. He just stood there, staring down and motionless. His beady eyes fixed on Duncan as Duncan dragged himself away from the stairs until his back hit against the wall, stopping him from going further. The clown laughed again but, his laughter stopped abruptly as though the joke were no longer amusing.

Through the pain in his ankle, Duncan yelled up the stairs, 'What do you want?!' The clown didn't respond, merely clenched his fists into tight balls. What he wanted was to kill Duncan. He wanted to rip the man's head off and boot the severed head straight through one of the boarded windows, to the crowds below but he couldn't. If they made it down the stairs, however they got there, that was where his domain ended. Those were the rules to make it more exciting for those outside and to give those inside more of a fighting chance, not that they really had any.

The clown turned away and stomped back down the landing. Soon after, a door slammed shut. And there he would remain until the next guest entered the property.

For a moment Duncan didn't move. He just stayed there, on the floor, slumped back against the wall and unsure whether the clown really was gone. There was a part of him which believed he was simply being toyed with and, any minute now, the clown would reappear and run down the stairs towards him, laughing with each step of his over-sized shoe. Duncan wasn't the only one to have stopped in his tracks.

Outside, Erin had stopped talking to Laura and the others standing with them. She was staring up at the screen apprehensively. Until this moment, she had belief that "her man" would get the furthest but - the night-vision clearly picked up his broken ankle. Even if it hadn't, there was no mistaking the audible "crack" which popped through the system's speakers.

David laughed. 'He only has himself to blame.'

'What are you talking about?' Erin asked.

'He broke his own ankle. No one else did. He fucked himself,' David explained.

Bob took a swig of his beer and said, 'We'll see.'

The house was challenging enough without having to navigate it with a broken bone. 'Get up,' she mumbled to herself.

There was no way Duncan had heard her. Confused with what was going on, he knew he was in the derelict house and he realised everything was a sick game but, he didn't realise *how* sick it was. Nor did he know why they were playing the game on him, or how far they would go to "scare him". As, to him, that's all they were trying to do at this particular moment. With a broken ankle, he figured the game was over and, any minute now, they'd come bursting in - laughing at his expense, until they clocked his ankle. Then they'd probably all rally around, desperate to help out and make sure he was okay. Or rather, to make sure he wasn't about to sue them which, at the moment, was pretty high up on his list of "wants".

'I think it's broken!' he called out, unsure as to whether they realised the extent of his injury. When no response came, he called out again, 'You hear me?' Still nothing. 'Fucking arseholes,' he spat. With the realisation dawning on him that no one was coming, he pulled himself up from the floor, using the battered wall to steady himself. There was just one door at the end of the hallway he found himself in. With the exception of the back wall he was leaning upon, the two main walls leading to the doorway were lined with mirrors. The only light, offering him a view of where to go, came from a flickering bulb overhead. With no other choice, he knew he had to go through the door at the far end. 'Shit,' he muttered.

Duncan put the hand - on the same side as his broken ankle - onto the mirror and, with his fucked foot raised off the floor, he hopped down the corridor towards the closed door ahead. With each pained "step", he wasn't sure if he'd be thankful to see people standing on the other side of the door, ready to cheer him and laugh at how they scared him. Or, would he simply lunge at them and smack the closest person clean in the face?

As Duncan neared the door, one painful hop after one painful hop, he guessed he'd just surprise himself with what he'd do. *How could they think any of this was funny?* But then, he figured it was similar to that "haunted house" experience in the States. Apparently that place was so extreme, no one made it through without quitting. And, according to the reports, some people even passed out in there, although Duncan read those "reviews" with a pinch of salt. For all he knew, they were just bullshit marketing gimmicks. That being said, the people who entered that haunted house? They had volunteered themselves for it. Given how one minute Duncan had been drinking outside, and the next he was in here - he was hardly a volunteer. If anything, he was a prisoner.

13

David laughed as, on screen, Duncan burst through the next door. The idiot even stumbled over his bad ankle and fell to the floor when the shotgun, hanging close to the wall, "clicked". Had it been re-loaded from earlier, Duncan would have been another fatality.

'I know Laura's contribution didn't get very far but, got to be said, I don't think yours is anything special,' David said. Laura smiled. Whilst she secretly liked Erin, she wasn't ever overly impressed with how Erin thought she was better than everyone else. It was an ugly trait and so, when she was brought down a peg or two, it was pleasing to see. Of course, Laura never made her feelings clear and, as quickly as she smiled, she wiped the grin from her face.

Bob defended his daughter, 'Hey now, our guy made it further than your guy.'

'By luck. Had he gone in there first, he'd have been dead.' David wasn't wrong. The first contribution's brains and head pieces were still plastered on the wall like a fucked-up 3D decoration. It was a mess which hadn't gone unnoticed by Duncan, he was still - on screen - sitting on his arse, clutching his ankle.

Bob laughed. 'Everything in life is luck, is it not? The rich people in life are only there because of luck. Right place, right time. Luck or inheritance. That's what makes a rich person,' Bob said.

'Or skill,' David corrected him. 'Hard work...'

'Trust me, David, I know many people who are highly skilled in their craft, and hardworking, who are flat out broke because they haven't had the "luck" to be seen yet.' Bob continued, 'Anyone who gets out of that house... Lucky. Nothing more and nothing less. Just turns out we chose someone luckier than your girl did.' Bob turned to David and flashed him a shit-eating grin and a little wink. David just smiled back. There was no point in arguing with someone like Bob. The Bobs of the world were always right, even when they were wrong and knew it. They would entirely change their outlooks if it served a purpose to make them "right".

'Can you two please be quiet?' Erin said, unable to take her eyes from the screen. She knew Duncan couldn't survive the house. Even if he got out, he'd have to be killed. But that didn't mean she wasn't willing him to make it out of there. If he did, he'd be the first person to ever find the exit. *Her* man would be the one who got away. Well, momentarily. As per the agreement, they'd soon take him back in there and slit his throat so his blood seeped into the floor. Those were the rules.

Bob laughed at his daughter. 'Sounds like someone likes their contribution a little too much.' He asked outright, 'Did we get ourselves attached to him?'

The perfect answer to her teasing dad, Erin simply shrugged and said, 'What? He was good with his tongue.'

Bob pulled a disapproving face and tutted. 'Oh please.'

Again, Laura couldn't help but stifle a laugh. Not just because Erin had grossed her father out but also because she knew, if what Erin did was any sign of how Duncan performed, he *did* know what to do with his tongue. She wasn't exactly lying.

Duncan had pulled himself up to his good foot. Again, he was using the wall to steady himself and keep from putting his fucked foot down. With the exception of the shotgun hanging from the wall, with string going from trigger to door handle, the room was bare. Just as there was on the landing upstairs, and the room he'd woken in, there was a boarded window letting in a narrow slit of light. Other than that, there was another closed door leading to God only knew where. Unsurprisingly, Duncan wasn't keen to go through the door but, he also knew he had little to no choice.

Frustrated, and still convinced this was all a sick joke, he hobbled over to the door. He took a hold of the handle with a shaking hand and, carefully and out of direct blast-radius of any particular weapon on the other side, he twisted the handle and pushed the door open. There was no bang, there was no click. There was just a God-awful stench of rotten meat and the loud sound of flies buzzing around.

'What the fuck…'

Without going into the room, Duncan would see what looked like realistic human bodies pinned to the ceiling. From throat to stomach, they were sliced open. Their entrails hung from the open wounds; red strands of string-like tape which made it hard to see through to the other side of the room. Convinced it was all fake, Duncan still gagged thanks to the stink of rotting flesh. A smell which was made that much worse thanks to the warmer weather recently. A scent which reminded Duncan of passing by a butcher's shop on a hot summer's day.

Duncan told himself, 'It's just props.' He extended both hands in front of himself and hopped through. The first wet, slimy strand slapped him in the face and stuck in place. He let out a moan of disgust, pausing a moment to wipe his face clean. He told himself again, 'It's just props.' But it wasn't and, had he looked up, he would have recognised the "drunk man" being carried into the house earlier. He spat some of the "slime" out of his mouth, having accidentally getting some in there. With a strong, lingering taste of mince-meat, he told himself again, 'It's just props. They're just fucking with you…'

GIRL TEACHES BOY

14

BEFORE

Murray was visibly getting frustrated with Duncan's lack of drinking. Erin was standing next to him, just looking awkward but - other than that - there wasn't much more she could do, other than force the drink down his neck. That wasn't about to happen.

Duncan asked, 'What's the story with the house anyway?'

Murray immediately went on the defensive. 'What do you mean?'

'Well I can see it's derelict but, that's a good bit of land. With the other houses on the street, I'm surprised it hasn't been snatched up by a developer. Or even a private individual. Could either make this place good again or just flatten it and start again…'

'Oh, you're in property development?' Murray asked sarcastically.

'No. Just know a good deal when I see one. Anyway, I'm surprised you guys don't want it dealt with. Not exactly nice for your street, is it? Probably knocks some of the value from your own places…' Duncan was entirely oblivious to how offended Murray was getting. Erin wasn't.

Before Duncan could piss Murray off any further, Erin stepped in and asked, 'You really don't know what that place is?'

Duncan laughed. 'Other than a shit-hole?'

'Hans Ferrell lived there…'

Duncan's face dropped. He knew the name. Pretty much everyone in the country, at least those old enough to see the news, knew who Hans was. In fact, people all over the world knew the name. Although not from this country initially, Hans was considered one of the country's most prolific - and sadistic - serial killers. For years he'd lived, blending in with society as *Mr.*

Average. But, in his quiet home in a well-to-do area, he was butchering homosexual men.

Hans would pick his victims up in the gay clubs around town. He'd bring them back to his house under the guise of wanting to have intercourse with them but, once they were locked in his home, his true intentions were quick to come to light. First, he would drug them. Then, he'd put them into bed where he would leave them to wake up. Once they did, their first instinct was to run. They'd leave the room but find the house had been turned into a maze. Unable to find the way out, Hans would toy with them until he grew bored. At that point he'd appear before them, chainsaw in hands. Blade spinning.

'*The* Hans Ferrell?'

Erin nodded.

'Well now I'm even more surprised they didn't just knock the place down *and* that you guys didn't try and capitalise on this... You know how many people would pay good money to have a look in that house? Or to stay in there? You're letting it fall to ruin, but you could be making a fortune! Especially if you opened it up on Halloween as a horror-maze.'

Murray turned to Erin and sarcastically asked, 'Why didn't we think of that?' Erin replied with a look.

A sudden thought crossed Duncan's mind. When they had finally discovered Hans identity, the police had surrounded his house. To their surprise, he came out both naked and brandishing a buzzing chainsaw. He was splattered with gore and ranting like an animal. They shot him dead on the spot. 'Did you guys see him get killed? When the police shot him?' That was his question; not whether they suspected what was going on just a few doors down from where they lived. Without waiting an answer, he shook his head and said again, 'What a wasted opportunity…' With that, he took a swig from his beer. He immediately pulled a face. 'Ergh. I think it might be off.'

Erin laughed. 'It's not "off". One of the neighbours always brings the cheap foreign beers.' She turned to Murray and said, 'Did you really give my boyfriend one of the cheap beers?'

Murray shrugged.

Erin said to Duncan, 'Just down it and I'll get you a proper one to wash away the taste.'

Duncan laughed. 'Sounds like a plan to me.' He put the bottle back to his lips and, as instructed, he proceeded to down it. Faster it was gone, faster he could get a better drink. Preferably one which didn't take like medicine.

'Well cheers,' Murray said as a smile finally spread across his face.

Duncan fell through the open doorway and landed painfully on his ankle in the next, narrower room. The pain in his ankle throbbed through the rest of his body and caused him to scream out in pain.

'Enough already! You're fucking aware I've broken my ankle, aren't you? Just... *Enough*!' He paused a moment, listening out. Deeper in the house now, he couldn't even hear the muffled music from outside. How in the hell a crumbling house could be so well sound-proofed, he had no idea. 'Hello? Can you even hear me?' There was no answer. 'You realise this isn't funny, right?' In his mind, this was all still a practical joke from the people who'd invited him to the party. They were just toying with him. A "tradition" they enjoyed every year. He was half-right. Whilst they were toying with him, to those watching - this wasn't a joke.

With pain, Duncan got up to his knees. The room was spinning around him as his ankle continued to throb. His vision was tainted with stars. As the room momentarily blurred, he couldn't help but wonder whether they'd come for him if he passed out, or whether they'd just leave him there until he came too and carried on trying to find his way out.

In front of him, there were two doors. Written in what looked like reddish-brown paint, the letter "A" was on one door and, "B" was on the other. Clearly a choice he had to make. When he was ready, that was. For now, he was happy to kneel here and regain his composure or, at the very least, convince his body not to let him faint from pain.

As he was kneeling there, his mind drifted to those who'd been in this position before him. Not guests of the fucked-up party, making their guests look like idiots but people who had actually been brought back to the house by Hans, when he was alive. What they must have been feeling and thinking. The fear and terror of not knowing what was going on and then - that feeling amplified when Hans appeared before them, armed with his chainsaw. The thought made Duncan feel sick, or was that also the pain?

A little voice in his mind pointed out the pain wouldn't be stopping anytime soon, not unless he got up and out of the house. He dragged himself over to the wall and, using the tried and tested method, he pulled himself up to his good foot.

The question was: A or B?

THE BOYS BEFORE

15

BEFORE

Stuart danced his way across the nightclub's crowded dance floor, back over to the bar where he was pleased to see the man was still sitting. As he reached the stranger, he gave him a playful pat on his arse and said, 'Honey, I'm back. Did you miss me?' He confessed, 'Honestly I was hoping you were going to follow me to the toilet. When you didn't, I was just hoping you hadn't taken the opportunity to run out on me.' He laughed as the stranger - David - turned around.

David laughed. 'Run out on you? No. But, sadly, I do have to leave. I've got an early start in the morning.'

'Oh? Doing Mayor things?' Stuart teased.

David laughed again. 'I'm going to have to get a photo of this David guy, aren't I? I get mistaken for him a lot but as you saw from my driving licence, it is definitely not me.' True enough, David had shown a driving licence to prove to the stranger that he wasn't the Mayor, but just a random lookalike. Obviously, the licence was fake and, if a person looked close enough, they'd be able to tell that. Still, in the dim lights of the gay bars, it was good enough to pass the test and avoid any awkward moments. David - or Richard as stated on his licence - said, 'I wonder if being a lookalike pays well? I might have found myself a second job.' He laughed, as did Stuart.

'Do you really have to go?'

'Afraid so but, if you give me your number - I'll call you?'

'Promise?'

David nodded. 'Sure.' He wasn't sure when he could sneak out on another "business dinner", having had so many recently, but - for Stuart, a handsome man in his twenties with dark hair and baby blue eyes, he'd find the time. If only for a lunch date someplace quiet where he could suck him off without any prying eyes nearby. David tried to shake the image from his head. The last thing he wanted was to get himself turned on just as he had to go. He took out his mobile phone and handed it to Stuart. 'Here, put your number in.'

Stuart smiled and, as requested, tapped his digits into David's device. 'You will call me, right? Don't leave me hanging.'

'I promised, didn't I?'

Stuart handed the phone back to David and warned him, 'You'd better. Otherwise I'll march straight down to the mayor's office…'

David laughed. 'Not sure that will do you any good but, okay.' He got up from the bar stool and pocketed his phone. 'Well, Stuart, it was nice to meet you and I wish our evening didn't have to end so abruptly.'

So did Stuart. 'And it was nice to meet you too, Richard.'

David confirmed again, 'I'll call you.' Then, he turned away and walked towards the stairs which led a winding path up to the bar's exit. Not ready to call it a night yet, Stuart sat on the vacated stool and called the bartender over.

'Vodka on the rocks,' he said.

The bartender nodded and proceeded to get Stuart's drink as Stuart looked back over to the stairs, hoping to see David heading back to him. No such luck. David was gone. Stuart sighed with disappointment, oblivious to the fact he was being watched from the other side of the dance floor.

Hans stepped from the shadow.

Stuart stumbled from the bar's fire exit and fell into the alleyway. The only thing which stopped him from hitting the deck was the fact he had fallen against the building opposite the bar. Had he been sober, it might have hurt but, as it was, he couldn't help but to laugh and call himself a, 'Fucking idiot.'

A voice startled him from behind as it asked, 'You okay?'

Stuart turned to see who was standing behind him with such a "cute" accent. Hans.

'You didn't hurt yourself?' Hans asked. He was standing in the same doorway Stuart had just stumbled from. A look on his face of fake concern for the drunken man.

'Take more than that to hurt me,' Stuart boasted.

Hans smiled. In his mind he was already picturing exactly what it *would* take to hurt him, or any of the other poofs dancing their night away.

Stuart pushed himself away from the wall and started to sway down the alleyway, towards the main street. Hans watched for a while, then followed.

'Where are you going?' Hans asked.

'I am going home!' Stuart said in a very drunk matter of fact tone. Little did he know, it wasn't the booze which had made him like this. Watching strangers dancing on the dance floor, wishing he were a part of their party, he'd taken his eye off his drink for just a split second. That was all it took. Within fifteen minutes of finishing the beverage, the room was spinning and his legs felt wobbly beneath him. Surprised at how drunk he was feeling, that was when he decided to call it a night…

'But it's still early,' Hans said. 'Be a shame to end the evening so early, wouldn't it?'

Stuart paused in his step. For a moment he stood there, swaying, as he processed Hans' words. Slowly he turned back to the stranger and asked, 'Are you flirting with me?'

Hans smiled. 'My car is just around the corner, and I don't live too far from here if you'd like somewhere warm and comfortable to sober up.'

Stuart frowned. It was a weird way of being propositioned for a fuck - at least that was what he thought was happening - but he shrugged it off. From the man's accent, he was clearly not from around here so… Fuck it. 'Now that sounds like more fun than I had lined up for myself. Did you know I was going to go home and watch some porn?'

Hans laughed, despite feeling repulsed inside. In his mind he pictured this dirty cunt fucking his hands whilst watching two guys suck and fuck one another. Keen to get him to come back, Hans swallowed his pride and said, 'Well… We can always keep the porn a part of your evening's plans.'

Stuart laughed and covered his mouth in mock-shock. 'Oh my! How rude…. I hope you're not thinking we can watch porn together and fuck. I'm not that sort of man,' he joked. 'No. We can watch porn and make love…' He laughed again. 'Lead the way, my sexy man.'

As the two men walked down the alleyway, now in the opposite direction to the main street, Stuart had no idea that - by morning - he would be just another statistic.

16

Stuart woke, naked and with a start. Confused, he looked around the unknown room. He frowned, unsure as to how he got there. The last thing he remembered was drinking at the bar of his favourite establishment. Had he got lucky? The room was nice enough. Plush carpets, nice bedding, decent furniture. At least he hadn't ended up in some dosshouse. No sign of whoever he'd come back with though. Maybe whoever it was had given up the bed for them, realising he was too drunk when they got him home? It made sense. Otherwise, they'd be lying on the other side of the bed now, sleeping.

Without wanting to walk around someone else's home without them knowing about it, Stuart called out,

'Hello? Sorry… I must have passed out. Guess I drank too much.' He laughed nervously. 'I didn't even think I'd had that much.' When there was no answer, he called out again, 'Hello?' Still no answer.

Stuart turned back to the bed. He expected to see his clothes screwed up on the floor but, there was no sign of them. He frowned. Maybe he'd thrown up on himself and his mystery guest had gone and put them in the wash? That was generous of them but, he couldn't let them do it. Not without offering to help at least.

Stuart opened the bedroom door and looked out to the landing. With no light switched on, and the night sky beyond the window, the landing space was dark. Stuart resisted the urge to call out again. Without knowing who was living here, he didn't know if there was anyone else in the house, who *didn't* know he'd come home. Christ, imagine standing here naked and having a kid come jump out. Not sure who'd be more surprised, or scared.

Stuart listened for the sound of movement from anywhere but, there was none. Quietly, he crept towards the top of the stairs. There, he listened again but - this time - concentrating on movement from downstairs.

Still nothing. The house was still and eerily silent. Stuart's next thought - that he'd broken into a stranger's empty house was stupid yet, there it was. Right at the forefront of his tired mind. It wouldn't be the craziest thing he'd done when drunk. Even so, he thought he was past that stage of his life now. But then, he hadn't got *so* drunk in a long, long time so God only knew what he was capable of.

Unconvinced that the house was empty, and that he had broken in, Stuart quietly crept down the stairs. He half expected to find someone down there, crashed out on the living room sofa. A perfect gentleman. Stuart just hoped that, when he saw the homeowner, he'd remember the person's name. Otherwise, that could make for an awkward conversation. Well, an even more awkward conversation. As it was, he wasn't entirely sure if they'd *done* anything. Although, if they had, he could at least tell he hadn't been the one who'd received. Not "back there" anyway.

At the bottom of the stairs, Stuart jumped at his own reflection staring back at him in one of two mirrors on the hallway wall. He laughed at himself, for being such a dick and, he walked to the door at the end of the hallway. A weird set up, he thought. He'd expected a front door, a door to a kitchen, a dining room, a living room, maybe a study area but - nope - there was just one door. With no other options, he opened the door. He frowned. Another empty room with just one more door leading to whatever waited behind.

'What the fuck is this place? Damn maze!'

As he made his steps towards what would be the last room he'd ever see, Stuart had no idea that he was being watched via unseen cameras. His viewing audience wasn't the man who owned the house. His viewer lived a few doors down.

The chainsaw blade spun to life with an almighty buzz the moment Duncan opened "Door A". Before he had a chance to react, the chomping teeth were pushed against his stomach. In the blink of an eye - and with the chainsaw's petrol engine drowning out the screams - the sharp teeth immediately started eating into his flesh first, and then his intestines. Blood and gut juice sprayed over the chainsaw-wielding maniac, and the surrounding walls.

A MAN'S PLAN

17

David watched the giant screen as Duncan was cut in two. Despite the gore on display, none of the neighbours turned away or even acted disgusted. Just as they always did, they clapped and cheered having become desensitised to it all.

Before Hans' death, these people had been watching these acts of violence from the comfort of their own homes on a regular basis, with David's promise that those who were being killed were the scum of the city. Dirty little cunts caught doing wrong; bringing society down and making the lives miserable of those who didn't deserve it. *Why spend your tax money keeping them fed and housed in prison when we could just kill them? Lower crime rates, lower tax hikes and - on the plus side - some entertainment and satisfaction in watching someone get what they truly deserve.*

Watching now, David couldn't help but to smile at what he had helped create, and keep running long after Hans' death. A "kill club" with his fellow neighbours successfully brainwashed into thinking it was for "the good of the city", despite the truth being - it was never actually about the "bad people" getting what was deserved, or making the city a better place. The people brought to the house by Hans weren't the criminals they were painted out to be. They were just normal people, living their lives up until the point they met the wrong person. Still, David's accomplices didn't need to know that. Although David did occasionally wonder how many people knew this to be the truth and were just happy to turn a blind eye. Especially since Hans' death when it was the daughters going out and bringing victims home. Just normal boys looking to date and get laid. No criminals, no deserved deaths… Just entertainment and the chance to win money by placing a lucky bet. No one seemed to care. With regards to the bets, they all knew the chance of winning money was next to nothing. They didn't care. It was still a thrill to try and "win".

'Shit!' Erin said. She took a betting slip from her jacket pocket and ripped it in two. Her father, Bob, turned to her with anger in his eyes. Clearly he'd bet heavy on his daughter. 'Sorry, daddy.'

David laughed. He wasn't surprised at the outcome. He'd known Erin's competitor had been nothing more than a sack of bone and shit the moment the dumb idiot fell down the stairs and broke his own ankle. He was glad the guy didn't end up proving him wrong.

'That it, or do we have any more?' Murray called out from over by the drinks table. As the group continued to discuss what else was to come, David couldn't help but to take a step back and just watch them all in action. From the moment he had watched Duncan spill his guts onto the floor, the smile hadn't left his face. Watching his neighbours, enjoying their yearly night of carnage and mayhem, his smile continued to grow. One thing was for sure, they'd come a long way from when Hans used to broadcast his kills to their homes.

BEFORE

David leaned forward in his office chair and moved his face closer to the computer screen of his laptop. There was a wide grin on his face as he watched Stuart beg and plead for his life. Hans was standing over him; a bloody knife in his hand which had already been pushed into Stuart's stomach more than a couple of times.

Stuart was on the floor. His hands were outstretched towards Hans. Tears streamed down his face as the gravity of his situation weighed down heavily on him. Hans felt no empathy. He just laughed in the defenceless man's face and - then - slashed across it with the knife. Stuart fell back and put his hands to his bleeding face as he screamed in pain. Aware that his family was in the other room close by, David turned the sound down on his computer.

They always targeted homosexuals. Hans hated them and described them as being a plague on humanity. David's reasons for wanting to hurt them were far different. He was jealous of them. They lived the live he secretly desired for himself. They didn't seem to feel the same shame he felt. They hadn't got themselves caught up in a marriage, even with a kid in tow now. They were free to do what they wanted and how they wanted and, seemingly, without a care in the world. David hated that. Why should they be so happy when he couldn't be? Of course, when he spoke to Hans he hid this side of himself, just as he did from everyone else too. He buried it deep and, instead, pretended just to hate.

Hans said to Stuart, 'You disgust me.'

'Please, I haven't done anything…'

'But you have,' Hans said. With a gloved hand, he reached down and grabbed Stuart's flaccid prick. Stuart flinched at the grab but wasn't in any position to do anything about it. He just wept through the pain and fear; the knowledge he was going to bleed out if he didn't get any help soon, the knowledge that he wasn't going to see his family again.

Hans stretched Stuart's cock away from his body and started to hack at it with the knife. The pitch in Stuart's scream changed the more his member was hacked at until his mouth was open but no sound was audible to humans. Hans laughed harder as he pulled the *almost* severed member away. Just a few strings and strands of flesh desperately trying to keep the two things attached to one another. Hans gave one final tug and they released their grip and - the dick was severed. Stuart slumped down on the floor, onto his side. His mouth still open, with no human-audible sound coming from it. Hans took the opportunity to give Stuart a little treat in his final moments on this planet. He shoved Stuart's severed cock into his mouth and down the back of his throat, laughing as he did so. As Stuart choked to death, Hans rose to his full height and turned to the camera hanging from the ceiling. He gave it a little wink as if to tell the viewers, *Another one done.*

With the show over, David closed his laptop down. He leaned back in his chair and sighed. Usually he'd be thinking about the killing for a few days at least. Tonight though, he was just wishing he'd been "forced" to have a prick in his mouth. With such thoughts in mind, he knew he wouldn't be able to wait the usual amount of time they gave it between killings, or else he'd just keep imagining what it would be like to suck on a dick. To get the image from mind, he needed to watch someone else suffer and - with any luck - Hans wouldn't do "that" again, having hopefully got it out of his system with Stuart. *What was he thinking? He'd never done that before...*

David's phone, sitting on his office table, pinged through with a new message. Curious, David picked the phone up and clicked to see what he'd been sent. It was one of his neighbours laughing about the show. *Fucking hell, that was brutal! More like that please LOL Give them what they fucking deserve.*

The police cars circled the house at the end of the street. Armed officers jumped out of their vehicles and surrounded the building with weapons aimed, and ready. With all the commotion and the brightness of the blue lights flashing, the neighbours came out to see what was going on, even though they knew. None more so than David. It was his fault they were there after all.

The government had always known what was happening in the house. They knew of Hans, they knew of the broadcasting to the rest of the street. They turned a blind eye because they took payment; payment which went into running their campaigns and keeping them in power. Had they shut the neighbourhood down, they would have also been hypocrites as they weren't unfamiliar with such antics themselves. The difference between what David had set up to that they'd done? David's "fun times" were on a much smaller scale.

Tucked away in the countryside, a massive compound had been built for the sole purpose of running experiments on people. Experiments which, nine times out of ten, resulted in death. It was - the Prime Minster told his people - for the good of the country and, that's exactly what David had told him about the house too, and Hans. The bullshit excuse that they were just "taking out the trash". The Prime Minister didn't give a shit so long as it *was* the trash. People not willing to put something into society, play their part in making the country good were, the Prime Minister believed, better off dead. David assured him it would only be the law-breakers who were taken to the house and, he also promised monthly payouts too. The Prime Minister signed off on it but warned him, if it ever came to light - he would deny everything and he would shut it down with extreme force. David agreed.

The police were here now because David had approached the Prime Minister. He told how Hans had gone off the rails and was just taking anyone into the house. He didn't mention the fact it was mostly homosexuals and neither did he mention Hans' new interest in severing the dicks off the men; something which was now happening with *every* kill. He'd cut their penis off and shove it in their mouths, forcing them to choke to death as he took up his chainsaw. The problem was, every time he did it, David could only think about having a dick shoved in his mouth. The kills became a faded memory in his mind and his days were consumed with homosexual thoughts again. The whole point of these kills was to put such thoughts from his mind, but encourage them. *He knew he had to betray Hans.*

David watched from the edge of his drive as Hans came out of the house brandishing his chainsaw. Some of the neighbours were looking at David, worried that they'd be linked to what happened in the house but, David wasn't stressed. He'd made sure, with another kickback, that it was only Hans who was going to go down for this. They had nothing to worry about. In fact, little did they know at this stage, nothing would really change for them. David already had a plan on how to keep this going, albeit once a year.

Hans ignored the cops' warnings. His chainsaw buzzed loudly, echoing down the road. He shouted for them to fuck themselves and - then - the officers opened fire. The moment his body hit the ground, David turned away and went back towards his house. Laura was watching from the doorway, scared but - again, along with the others - with nothing to really fear. As David reached her, he put his arm around her, and the pair disappeared back into the house. David closed the door. In the morning, when he'd hold a street meeting, he'd open another "door".

18

NOW

Murray's words, along with those he was talking to, had turned to noise as David zoned out to what they were saying. He was distracted with thoughts of the past and how they had all come to be here. The fact the group were discussing a "quota" was David's fault. When he had kept this going after Hans' death, he had informed them that the government had said it was fine so long as they kept to a certain number of "deletions" each year.

Deletions was how he referred to the criminal element being removed from society. He said it was the government's phrase but, along with the quota, that was a lie. Something which *was* true though, was the fact that he *had* struck a new deal with the government after Hans' death.

David told the Prime Minister that they'd have a party each year, at Hans' house (so it was imperative they didn't knock it down) and - at that party - they would delete a few more unsavoury characters from the society. The government would, of course, continue getting their payments - something they'd got since David first got the green-light from them - and David and his friends would continue satisfying their bloodlust. It was a win for all.

In the first few years, the daughters went to clubs and targeted the arsehole men; those who'd prey on drunk women. They'd befriend them, sometimes just lead them on - with a promise of a fuck on Halloween at "this party we've been invited to". Other times they just fucked them and kept fucking them until the time came for them to lead them to the house. The years went on and - at some point it became less about picking out the arseholes and more about just bringing *anyone* back. A worry hanging in the air that if they didn't bring someone back then they wouldn't reach the necessary quota the "government" had agreed to and, if that happened…?

David ensured the neighbours continued to be involved by warning them; *if the quota isn't reached then they said they'd arrest us and charge us for murder. We're committed to this for life now.* The truth was, he just didn't want the killing to stop. A thought that - actually - doing this made him more of a man… He wasn't the faggot… He *was a man*. That wasn't to say he was cured entirely. The homosexual thoughts, whilst muted, were still there. But now a heavy cloud of paranoia hung heavy over him. A very real worry that someone on the street would turn on him, just as he'd turned on Hans.

As a precaution he had the neighbours' phone lines tapped. He'd even installed hidden cameras here and there, filming into their properties. Even his own home was littered with recording devices as, he figured treachery could come from anyway. And *that* was how he discovered his daughter's secret…

Laughter rippled through the room. *He* stopped talking. An irritated look fell upon *his* face as he glared at others within the group.

'What's so fucking funny?' he asked, with his thick accent.

A BROKEN MAN

19

Hans glared at the others sitting with him. He asked again, 'What's so fucking funny?'

None of them dared to answer him. Despite the fact he was confined to a wheelchair, he still had a malevolent presence about him which made the other inmates uneasy.

'What, you going to fucking laugh at me for no reason?'

He turned his attention to the doctor who was sitting in the circle, more or less opposite where Hans' wheelchair had been parked. The doctor wasn't laughing. He was simply staring straight at Hans, waiting for him to complete his story.

'You wanted me to talk, I talk. I talk and these fucking clowns laugh at me. What's so fucking funny about what I'm saying?' Hans asked.

The doctor took a moment to think of all that he had heard this afternoon. Then, he recapped, 'So you were acting in conjunction with the whole street. And that included the Mayor and all his neighbours?'

'It's what I fucking said, wasn't it?'

'I see. And the Mayor is doing this because... Well... Now he does it to make himself feel more like a *real* man. The killing makes him less... Less homosexual?'

'That's right.'

'And before that, when you were doing all the killings and broadcasting it to their homes... The Mayor was doing it because he was a repressed homosexual and he'd instructed you to kill only the queer community because he was jealous of their freedom? He couldn't come out because of his job? Is that right?'

'Of course he couldn't. He's the Mayor. He'd lose the vote.'

'Because he's a homosexual?'

'People say they're fine with that kind of thing now but they're not. Not really. They'd vote for someone else to take over as Mayor…'

'I mean, before, you might have been right but times have changed…'

'Now they have. But we were doing this years ago and attitudes were very much different back then.'

'And you were happy to kill the homosexuals because…'

'I fucking hate them.'

'Any reason?'

Hans shrugged.

The doctor asked him direct, 'Have you ever had any thoughts about being with another man?'

'What? Why in the fuck would I think like that? It's fucking sick. You're fucking sick for asking. That, and stupid.'

The doctor said nothing. Over the years since he had been admitted to the mental health facility, Hans story had changed. Once upon a time he was working alone, then he was working with a number of individuals as part of a cult and - now - he was working with his neighbours, and the Mayor no less. Furthermore, the Mayor was apparently addicted to the killings and had turned Hans' house into a funhouse and, every year, they held parties there and kept killing.

Hans looked around at his fellow inmates. They were all laughing still. Most of them knew why the doctor asked such a question. David's thoughts were Hans' thoughts. David secretly liked men. Hans did. David didn't know how to handle the confusion in his mind. Hans handled it with rage and violence.

'Can you tell these cunts to stop laughing at me?' Hans continued. Hans changed the subject back to what he had been initially talking about, 'Anyway you interrupted me. *They* interrupted me with their stupid fucking laughing. I was about to tell you that, David knew his daughter and her friend, Erin, were lesbians. This reignited the rage within him and, you know what he did? He put *them* in the fucking house too… Not on clean-up duty but, to fucking survive it…' The group laughed harder still as Hans' story became more and more twisted as he went on.

The doctor looked at the clock hanging on the white wall. He stood up and said, 'Well that's all the time we have for this afternoon, so we'll pick this up again tomorrow.' He looked around the rest of the group and said, 'It would be nice to hear from some new people tomorrow too.' Most of them looked down at the white floor, purposefully avoiding the doctor's eye contact. For the majority of them, they were happy enough to let Hans tell his stories rather than stand up and talk about their own.

As the doctor headed towards the exit, looking forward to his end of shift beer, Hans called out after him, 'We can talk more about the government facilities out in the woods too, if you want… Should hear what they're doing to prisoners out there… Once you realise that, you'll realise why it was easy for them to let David carry on doing what he does after I was brought in here…'

The doctor left the room through a secure door.

Hans called out, 'You hear me? You even listening?' When he realised the doctor wasn't coming back, he slumped back in his wheelchair. *They never believed him*. Much to David's relief as, word *had* got back to him about how his name kept coming up in Hans' group therapy sessions…

'It's fine. He's in the funhouse. It's not like anyone takes him seriously,' one of the doctor's reassured David.

Made in the USA
Monee, IL
28 December 2025

40476057R00090